TATTERS

A Novella

Ash Ericmore

Written by: Ash Ericmore

Copyright © 2023 Ash Ericmore

All Rights Reserved. This is a work of fiction. No part of this publication may be reproduced, distributed, or transmitted in any form or by any means, except in the case of brief quotations embodied in critical reviews.

ISBN: 9798378596423

With Special Thanks to

Christina Pfeiffer, Leeanne Wright, August Vaughn, Christopher Ridge, Bameballs, and Eddie Greenham

Want to see your name here? Check out:

ko-fi.com/ashericmore/tiers

to find out how, as well as see all the other benefits of joining up.

For Caz

Chapter 1

In Trivialea Park there is a tunnel. It's a longish tunnel that used to take pedestrians from one side of the railway line to the other. That was when the railway line used to run there, through the park. Now the line is defunct and the tunnel is just another one of those tunnels that drug dealers use during the day to sell drugs to children.

And Harold uses it at night.

Even when Harold was a child his parents told him to never use the tunnel in the park after dark because it was scary and dangerous. And having seen it after dark, it was. Fucking scary, and surely fucking dangerous.

That is why he used it now. It helped to create the atmos.

Harold stood at the far entrance of the tunnel—depending on which side of the park you were on—just to the side of it, and waited. The old embankment rising, overgrown behind him, he waited for someone to come. A quick look up to the sky. The lights stopped you from seeing much, but the clouds were there, that was for sure. He was sure it was going to rain. He thought it before he left his flat.

He'd lived just outside the park for some five years now. In the basement of an old Victorian building, a flight of steps outside his front door leading straight to the pavement, on the other side of the road to the nice side of the park. The side where all the swings were. He could even remember there being a roundabout there when he was a kid, but that was gone before he moved in. Some cunt probably thought they were dangerous now. It wasn't like he ever heard of someone getting their arm ripped off or anything. Although he wouldn't have been surprised if someone had. He'd have to look it up online later.

He stuck his head out from the overgrowth and looked down the tunnel. There was someone coming. He could hear the footsteps. He'd done this enough times now that he could tell exactly where they were by their footsteps. They hadn't entered the mouth of the tunnel at the other end yet. But they *were* getting closer.

The tunnel itself was lit internally with electric lights on the ceiling that were about as powerful as tea lights. So once you were in the tunnel, you couldn't see much, which was just as well, because the tunnel was badly graffitied, and in Harold's opinion not really very pleasant.

Of course, you'd avoid it during the day, because of the drug dealers.

He walked through it himself, in order to get to this side of it, but that was okay. No one was going to mess with him, now were they? Harold shook his head. He could hear the patter of small dog feet now. Paws, that was the word. They were in the mouth of the tunnel at the other end. A dog walker. Good. Easy prey.

He stepped back, covering as much of himself as he could, without making a sound. Practised, as every motion he made was. Years of practice.

Harold breathed slowly. Quietly. The lull before the storm.

The footsteps coming closer.

Still as a mouse. Harold parted his lips slightly, transferring his breathing to there. He could hear his breath on the inside of the rubber nose when he breathed that way. Wasn't sure if the walker would be able to hear him or not, but he was sure the dog would. You have to be silent as a fucking vampire to get one over on a dog. He glanced down himself. Made sure everything was right.

His feet were sticking out.

Stupid fucking clown shoes. About four inches longer than his actual feet and he was a big guy. Big feet. Big everything. He grinned to himself. But he knew that was a lie, even in his own head. Not big ... everything. Anyway. Napoleon complex aside. He shuffled his feet back a little, making sure they didn't stick out past the edge of the bricks of the tunnel.

His round clown trousers didn't stick out as much these days. He'd taken them in, after finding that the council had stopped trimming these bushes and it was getting harder to hide in them. Being bushy, and all.

The footsteps were close now.

The dog made a yappy sound. Good. Small dogs are best. It would be on a lead. They always were, regardless, as at this time of night, with the dark tunnels and the shitty lighting, it was near impossible to find a dog that wandered off. Of late, Harold had started to notice that people were using those extendable leads more and more, but that didn't matter if it was a yappy dog. If it got too close he could always get his size twelve into it. Jab it away.

The footsteps were about to birth from the tunnel.

Harold straightened. He gripped his balloon tighter. Made sure he wasn't smiling, even though his white face was broken by a painted on demented smile.

The dog came from the tunnel first. It turned and looked directly at him.

Harold gulped. Waiting. Tense.

The dog flinched, like it might flee. Or fight.

Then the man came from the tunnel. Lanky. He was dressed in a light summer jacket. Slacks. An older man, balding, but not bald. Around eight inches shorter than Harold himself.

The dog growled, and the man looked down at it. He pulled on the lead. "Come on, Tatters," he said. "Leave Harold alone." Then he gently yanked the lead and Tatters wobbled off like a four-legged toddler, following its master into the night.

Harold watched. It wasn't the same anymore.

You know, a few years ago—shortly after Harold had moved there, being a clown in the bushes was a thing. It was important. You got attention, your face on, well, Facebook, and if you were really fucking lucky, maybe even a photo in the paper. Something shit, like a bigfoot photo. Gerald from Hampstead Heath was on the nine o'clock news once. But these days … well, it just wasn't the same.

People were no longer afraid of clowns staring.

A blob of rain landed on Harold's cheek and drooled down his face paint. He stepped out of the darkness and into the mouth of the tunnel, into a different sort of darkness.

Back through. Towards the flat.

He could hear the rain on the roof of the tunnel. His balloon dragging behind him.

CHAPTER 2

Harold sat in the Family Five, a local café off the industrial estate. He was stirring the tea that they'd put in front him, having chuted too much sugar into it from that shitty sugar dispenser these cafés had. The one with the funnel thing on top that you could never judge how much sugar was actually going to come out. He glanced up at the woman behind the counter. Not the one cooking but 'front of house,' if you could call it that, in a room little bigger than his living room that smelled of old fat and grease. Damn it, people used to respect him. He looked back into the brown swirlpool of the tea. The spoon chinking against the shitty china. He dropped it, rattling, to the saucer, resting his hand under his chin and looking at the wall. There was a laminated print out of a picture of a lasagne with *£4.99*, written in red underneath it. He'd had the lasagne once.

It was not good.

His eyes dropped back to the girl again. She couldn't have been more than twenty-five. Probably a little younger. Maybe. Maybe he was just getting older and couldn't tell the difference between a school girl and a young woman anymore. They all looked the same, didn't they? Kids today. Fuck. He shook his head and looked back into the tea. It was safe there. In the tea. She was pretty and he didn't want to stare.

"You need to take it to the next level."

Harold looked up at the clown sitting in the seat opposite him. He knew better than to answer him, because people had a tendency to look at him funny when he did. So he ignored the question and went back to the safety of his tea.

"You know. Take it up a notch."

He looked up again, so he'd know he heard. Nodded, and then went back to doing nothing, waiting for his all day breakfast. The clown that was sitting opposite him was called Howdy the Magnificent. At least, that was what he said his name was. Harold wasn't so sure. He thought that maybe Howdy had added the 'the Magnificent' on himself. He certainly didn't look magnificent. He was dirty. His face paint was applied covering every inch of his skin, perfectly, but then he'd looked like he'd been drinking heavily and sleeping in the gutter. Which, in all fairness, he smelled like, too. His yellow teeth showed when he spoke, and Harold had never seen him smile. His eyes were black. Like his pupils were far too big and the blue bit or brown bit—whatever that bit of the eye was called—just didn't show. Wore a yellow hat with a flower in it. A blue and yellow clown outfit. Regular human sized shoes. Another example of how un-magnificent he was. Couldn't even be bothered with proper clown shoes.

"Bring back the fear," he said.

Harold stayed staring at his tea. Then the woman—girl—whatever, came over. The front of house one, and slipped down his breakfast. He looked up. Honestly, she looked drop dead gorgeous, not that Harold would ever even consider asking her out. He smiled, silent, and then looked around the plate for his knife and fork. He didn't have one, but she was bringing them, so that was all right. She placed them down—they were wrapped in a black serviette—on the table and walked away without speaking.

"She's a rude cunt," said Howdy. "Imagine what

she'd look like if you put her in her place."

Harold slid his knife through the sausage, and wished he'd gotten a larger breakfast. One of each wasn't enough when he felt down. He kinda just wanted to eat, and eat, and eat. Until he was dead. He looked at the black pudding suspiciously as he placed the sausage in his mouth. Chewed.

"You could split her open and eat her guts."

Harold's chewing slowed. He looked across the café at the old man sitting in the window reading a paper, then back to the counter. The girl was making coffee or something. Her eyes flicked up to his when he looked at her, and he smiled, sausage still being slowly churned. He probably looked a bit retarded. She looked away and he kept looking. The thought of her lying on the table. Not this table. It was far too shit. But the table on the other side of the café. One against the wall, with that funny seating that's attached to the wall. An embonkment seat or something. It was a far sturdier table.

Laying, her uniform thing torn open. Naked beneath. A slit running from her throat down, in between her tits. Deeper below that, after the bone stops. Into her stomach. Blood pooling out the gash in her guts, up like a slow running geyser, and just as warm. Her intestines trailing out like the sausage he was cutting into.

He tore the uniform open a little more. He couldn't even fantasise about her properly. Too shy, he was. His mother had always said so. Now he'd torn her uniform open a little more he could see the hair in between her legs.

Harold stabbed his knife with too much vigour into his fried egg and the yellow stuff oozed out, over the white. He hurriedly cut a piece of the bread and butter and started to build a dam with it. Cutting more and more. He looked up. She was standing there watching him. She giggled, and went back to her coffee.

What was she laughing at? He wasn't dressed as a clown. Not now. He looked back at the table on the other side of the café. Plunged his fingers into her warm guts and started to pull them out. They stank so much he could almost taste them.

"That's right," said Howdy, "bring back the fear."

Harold snorted, looking at his breakfast. "It's not the same anymore," he hissed.

Howdy reached forward and picked up half a sausage and dipped it in the runny yolk. "I know," he said quietly. "I remember too, when we used to scare the bejesus outta people. Remember when Tony used to stand on the side of the M1 with his balloon and a dildo?" He tutted and sat back, munching his sausage.

Harold glanced up at him. "Mm." He looked to the girl behind the counter.

"You'll never get her like that."

He looked at Howdy. Frowned.

"I can see that look. You want her. I know. But no."

Harold focussed back on his breakfast, wiping things into the yellow of the egg, mopping it up and shovelling it in his mouth. He wanted out now. Enough of this conversation. As soon as he'd eaten enough to not seem wasteful he gulped back some coffee and then stood, leaving Howdy there. He went to the counter and paid.

He thrust his hands into his pockets as he left the café, the rain clouds covering the sun leaving the narrow road dark and unwelcoming. Howdy hurried up beside him. "You can bring the fear back, you know." Harold ignored him and continued on his way. Back towards the flat.

He needed to get ready for work.

Chapter 3

The cold in the air didn't make it any easier. He looked at the caterpillar on the stem of the rose bush. It wiggled forward and writhed around the thorn. Harold assumed it knew what it was doing, and left it be.

He wasn't very good at his job, but the people who employed him seemed dimmer than he was, so it didn't seem to matter. He thrust the small fork into the soil and turned it hard, clockwise, the roots of the weed coming free, so he could pull it out and drop it in the bucket next to him. He straightened his back and felt the usual burning ache that he got after being on his hands and knees too long. Pushing himself to his feet, he took the hoe and started to brush leaves about. It was going to be Halloween soon. Maybe he should do something special for that? Something to *... bring back the fear?*

He sighed, wondering if Howdy was wrong and it was just a phase. He was going to try again. Maybe one last time. See if he could drum up some of the old magic. He was the last of them, you know. Most of the old-time clowners had moved on to new things. Had jobs and girlfriends. Some of them started a band, he recalled. Something to do with jugglers, or something.

One last time.

It wasn't the first time he'd decided to do it one last time, but this time was different. *Yes.* He was going to go out there and scare someone. Scare them enough that he'd be *back*. Just like the old days. He looked down at the leaves. Danny was watching him from the other side of the rose plot. He had a toy gun in his hand. Just staring at him. "What you doing, Danny?" he called over. Best to be polite, although Harold was at his happiest when there was no need to interact with any of the family. Apart from Mrs. Cundray. She paid him in cash before he left. So that was a reason. Also, and it wasn't really for him to say, but she was *hot*. So there was that. He was still watching Danny, who hadn't moved. He stooped down and collected the leaves at his feet and pushed them down into his bucket. Danny moved around the bushes and stood there. Only a few feet from Harold. "What's up little man?" he asked. He pulled a cigarette butt from the soil and looked at it. Where the fuck were these all coming from? They weren't doing the flowers any good at all.

He'd been doing this house for some years and had known Danny more than half his life, but for some reason Danny always seemed a little distant. A little reticent to get involved. He always looked worried.

Then Danny shook his head, and turned, taking off running back towards the house.

Little psychotic weirdo.

One day he was going to say something to the Cundray's and that was going to be the end of it. Little bugger was going to go back to the house and say that Harold had put a worm in his trousers or something. There wouldn't be an investigation or anything, and Harold would be out on his ear, so to speak, just like that.

He picked up his bucket and headed over to the wheelbarrow. Emptied the bucket into the barrow and took it to the bins down the side of the house. The contents then went into the green wheelie bin, before he headed back to the centre of the garden. The grass needed a trim, but that would have to wait until next week.

Harold loaded the tools back into the wheelbarrow and took it back to the garage. Unlike some of the houses he did, the Cundray's had their own tools and for some reason preferred him to use those.

Then he went to the back door and knocked.

The door was unlocked, and he knew he was welcome to let himself in, but you know. No one likes to just help themselves, do they?

A moment passed before Mrs. Cundray came to the door. She was wearing a black dress thing that wrapped around her. Showed off her curves. The neckline plunged down *almost* too far, and Harold made sure not to stare. It wouldn't be the first time he'd had to hide a popped chubby in public.

"All done, Mrs. Cundray," he grumbled, looking anywhere but at her.

"Thanks, here," she said, holding out an envelope with his cash in. Cash was good. It meant he didn't have to declare all of it. The ice in the glass in her other hand clinked against the side of it. She always seemed to have a drink in her hand. Lush.

He reached out, taking the money, backing slowly away.

"Can I get you a drink or anything?" she asked.

Harold shook his head, bravely raising his eyes to meet hers. He did his best to smile and look polite, but he was burning. Nothing in his life was going right and … and … he stopped his brain from turning the thoughts over. He shouldn't be jealous of what everybody else had, should he? He shook his head still, turning away, and heading back towards the side of the house. Besides. He was going to show them. Then they'd be interested in him for who he was. He reached the front of the house, and hurried a little quicker, back towards the car. Sighing when he saw Howdy sitting in the passenger seat. Fuck. He thought he'd left for the day.

A glance back to the house and he saw Danny there in the window.

Bring back the fear.

The words bounced around in his head. He stumbled, managing to stay on his feet. Howdy grinning manically at him.

Bring back the fear.

Harold stopped, his face level with Howdy's sitting in the car, staring through the glass.

Bring back the fear.

Harold pulled away from him. His weird maniacal grin. He turned, leaning against the car, Danny, standing in the window. Harold raised his hand to wave and the little shit flipped him off.

So, he turned back to the car. Empty. Got in the driver's side, his fingers almost shaking too much to get the keys in the ignition. Stupid antique car. Why couldn't he have one of those cars that didn't need a key? He managed to jam it in and twist. The engine started.

"What are you, a fucking pedo?" Howdy turned his attention out the window, back towards the house.

"Fuck you," Harold blurted. The wheels spun to life. Around on the gravel, the car wanking into motion. Screaming out into the road. Harold banging his hands on the wheel saying *fuck you, fuck you.*

Fuck you.

Chapter 4

Harold pushed the paint around his face, smearing it into the corners of his hairline. It was getting harder to find the corners these days. His hair thinning slightly. He moved the paint around like a master these days, having applied it so many hundreds of times. Then he put the pot down, and picked up the red. To his eyes. He made a mental note to order some more of the grease paint from Amazon.

When he'd finished making himself up, he looked in the mirror with some admiration for the job he'd done. Howdy standing the room behind him. "It's no good," he said. "It won't work." He snorted, hawked up a loogie. "It's weak." He stood there rolling the phlegm around in his mouth before swallowing it back. "You're weak."

"I can do it again." Harold turned around, facing the monster. "I can make people afraid."

"You can't. Not like that." He picked up the brandy bottle from the corner and expertly flicked the lid, spinning it off. He took a swig and placed the bottle down.

Harold went over and crouched at his feet, retrieving the cap and putting it back on the bottle, taking it from Howdy. "I'll show you." He pulled a balloon from the pack and attached it to the gas cylinder, filling it, before tying a string off on it and letting it bob to the ceiling.

"Waste of fucking clown makeup, you are." Howdy's voice slurred.

Harold shook his head. This *was* going to work. He took the balloon and went to the front door.

Slipping his head out into the night. Making sure no one was coming, before he headed off into the park. He ran across the grass, laughing maniacally, as was his desire to do, a practised laugh, enough to terrify anyone who saw. Or so he thought.

Harold stood at the end of the tunnel. It was too late and too dark to get a dog walker tonight. He was going to get someone coming home from the pub. Some drunk. Maybe a couple, young, hanging off each other, very much in love.

And he was going to scare the living shit out of them.

Harold smiled to himself, pushing the leaves and sticks and dog shit around with his oversized shoe, making sure he could a) get far enough into his bush, and b) do it quietly. He reached back and snapped a couple of the branches so they wouldn't burst his balloon. Took a chance by creeping to the mouth of the tunnel and watching for a few minutes. Kept an ear on the sounds behind him.

Over the years he'd become adept at listening to the park. To *this* park. His park.

A laugh hung on the air. The wind carrying it for miles. An evil laugh, high pitched. It sent a shiver down Harold's back. Harold felt a pang of jealousy that a laugh like that could be scary. He watched, the shadows at the other end of the tunnel danced. Then he saw. Coming. A figure. It was impossible to tell at that distance whether it was a man or a woman. Didn't matter. He was going to scare them good. Show that fucker Howdy that you didn't need to do the things he made him see.

He watched the figure move, a second one coming into view. He could tell, by the way they moved, that they were both men. Harold frowned. Hm. A third, then.

He stayed well behind the bricks of the tunnel. Looking at the floor now. Shit. He didn't want any trouble. Harold looked back, away from the tunnel, deeper into the park. Then to the bushes. He was suddenly aware of what a bad idea this was.

The footsteps of the men getting louder in the tunnel, echoing like the drums of the dead. He pushed himself into his spot. Into the bushes. Further back. He had two choices. He could either be the scariest motherfucker in the universe.

Or he could run.

He looked at his shoes again. Running wasn't really part of the uniform was it? He could do this. He sucked air in and waited. Pushed himself back. If he was just visible enough then they'd be scared.

They were going to belittle him, weren't they?

No.

"Oh, yes." Howdy was standing on the other side of the tunnel arch. He looked down into the darkness.

"Shush," Harold hissed, waving him to get back and get out of sight.

But Howdy shook his head and watched them come. He looked back to Harold. "I think you're in trouble," he said. He squeezed his nose and it honked, cracking through the silence of the park.

"Bollocks," Harold whispered. Pushing himself further back. He could smell the dog poo. "Damn it." Maybe if he was far enough back they wouldn't see him at all. Then he could just wait for them to go away and he could go home. Maybe re-think his life. Ask that bird in the café if she wanted to go see a movie. Something about … not clowns.

The first of the men came from the tunnel. He

was a scrawny looking thing. Young, and wiry. Leather jacket and torn jeans. Were they back in fashion? Then the others came out. Harold wondered if the first one out might be their leader. Was that how gangs worked? He knew that was how gangs worked in school. You had a leader, right? And that song. Leader of the Gang or something. The gang leader was laughing at nothing in particular. And his friends seemed to be geeing him on.

"We could fuck one up," he said.

Harold didn't know what, neither did he care to know.

Howdy said, "You're fucked, you prick."

And then the leader of the pack (that was it) saw him. Harold. Standing in the bush, balloon above this head. Feet, sticking out and bit dog-shitty.

The four of them stood in silence for a moment, as the three of *them* looked at Harold and Harold tried to pretend he wasn't there. Maybe if he thought that hard enough the earth would just swallow him up.

Then the leader said, "What the fuck are you supposed to be?"

Harold wasn't sure if he was supposed to answer or not. Wasn't it obvious? So he just stared at them. Maybe he should try to scare them? He watched as they formed some sort of semi-circle around him. They seemed impressed.

Well, they looked like they were impressed. Harold smiled. Hoping they were going to go away.

The leader motioned Harold from the bushes. He wanted to speak to him. So Harold, a little less perturbed then, stepped out of the bushes and stood. Facing them. He wanted to go to the toilet. Quite badly.

"Are you supposed to be scary?" the leader said.

Harold nodded.

He put his arm around Harold's shoulders and pulled him in close. "Were you going to try and scare me?" He looked back over his shoulder to the rest of them. "Us?"

Harold looked at the three of them, one after the other. "No," he said, quietly.

"Are you sure?" The leader was nodding. A smile. Pleasant, like.

"Well," Harold dropped his head to the side, "maybe a little."

Howdy sucked air in through his teeth.

The leader, his head so close to Harold he could smell his brill cream, pulled his fist back and swiped it into Harold's gut. He didn't even see it coming. He hit him so hard he let go of his balloon. Harold doubled over, going down without too much fight. He felt sick, and his air was taken from him. He couldn't breath and everything hurt. He dropped to the floor, looking up into the night, seeing his balloon fly away. Leaving him.

Everything left him eventually.

Then he looked to the three of them. They were stood over him like he was a football. And like a football, they started kicking. Harold, rolled himself up as tightly as he could and tried to protect his face. He didn't care about being bruised, he just didn't want to lose his teeth. Pain wrapped around his ribs as one of them kicked him there, over and over, one in the stomach, he could taste the burning of puke rolling about in his throat, his back, spine being struck over. Over. Over.

He grunted out the pain, too afraid and too hurt to scream. With no air to help him. He tried to look, to see if he could see someone coming, running to his aid, but putting his head up just got him kicked in the face, the world suddenly turning white, spinning. As he tried to focus, white lights fired in his eyes like fireworks in the sky and this elongated howl like a siren ringing in his head, as he went slightly numb. He tried to beg, but there was nothing but pain. And a slow deathly feeling of parting with his body.

Then it all stopped.

He still breathed. In and out. Slowly. He could taste blood, his teeth loosed. His ribs bust, he was sure. This stinging pain when he breathed in. He was getting cold. Probably lying on the path. They were standing over him. Something landed on his face. Something wet. He was afraid to open his eyes. Not until he felt them move. He thought they might start to kick him again.

Muffled he heard one of them say they should go. And they did. Walking away into the night.

Leaving Harold lying there.

He waited. Something didn't feel right. It hurt to breathe. He reached up and touched his face, then looked at his fingers.

Blood.

Chapter 5

Harold opened his eyes, jerking awake. He lay on his bed. His guts stung. A fuzzy sting like he'd eaten too much and something inside him had popped.

Howdy was there. He was sitting on the other side of the room on a dining chair. Pushed it back onto the back legs. Like when you were a kid and your mum would tell you to *fucking well stop it*, or you'd fall backwards. Harold had, once. Fallen backwards. He was at school. Probably about eight or nine. He was sitting like that and he'd fallen backwards. Made a loud clatter and everyone looked. He'd rolled over and clambered to pick up his chair, embarrassed. Sat himself back down muttering something about sorry, when the girl sat behind him had made this urging sound, and someone else back there had started blubbing about something. His head had started to throb and when he'd reached back there it was warm, and wet, and sticky. The teacher had rushed over and looked him in the eyes like she was trying to see if someone was in there, and then he'd all but been ousted from the classroom. It was one of those portable classrooms, so out the door and to the playground.

That was the first time he'd seen Howdy, that day. He was sitting in the corner of the classroom when he'd pulled himself from the floor. Hadn't thought much about it at the time, but that could have just been his brain spinning around.

Howdy had looked different back then. Younger, and more alert. Less like a drunk bum who'd had a fight with a crack pipe and lost.

"Morning," he said.

Harold groaned and pulled himself from the bed. Sitting. He looked down himself, still in his clown outfit.

"Really brought back the fear, there, eh?" he continued.

"Go fuck a squirrel." Harold pushed himself up. His legs were weak. Out the bedroom, the room hot and sticky. Smelled of meat. He went to the kitchen and pulled his costume off. There was blood all down the front of it. "Fuckers," he grumbled. He pushed it in the washing machine and started the cycle, looking down at the wounds on his body. They'd closed up overnight, and stopped bleeding. Turning, Howdy was standing in the doorway behind him. Harold strode to him and pushed him out the way. Went to the bathroom and looked himself in the mirror. His makeup was smudged from where he'd slept, but was still firmly applied as it should have been. "That's the way," he said, smiling into the reflection. He poked at his gut wound and the stinging started again. Hungry. He returned to the kitchen.

"So what are you going to do about it? *Them*?"

He looked at Howdy. "What?" he said, opening the fridge. He stood, looking at the sparse foodstuffs, and breathed it all in through his nose, trying to decide what he wanted to have from there. It was none of it. He didn't want any of the bullshit food he had in the cupboard. He wanted to go to the café and get a full English.

Maybe.

"And you'll see her," he said.

"Fuck right off," Harold said, slamming the fridge door and storming to the living room. He sat, naked, on the sofa and picked up the TV remote, flicking on whatever shit was on British TV at that time in the morning.

Howdy sat in the armchair and watched the pictures as Harold flicked from one channel to the next. Harold could remember when there was only five channels and there was still more to watch on TV than there was now. He had some one hundred channels and half of them were just shit, and the other half all seemed to be catering for braindead moose. Mooses. Moosi? What. The. Fuck. Ever.

"You need to fuck them up," he said over the noise of the TV as Harold reached the adult stations that weren't showing anything at that time in the morning.

"I don't want to talk to you about it."

"I don't care. You know what needs to be done. Revenge. It's the next viable step, isn't it? Bring the fear, *while* getting revenge."

Harold squinted at the TV trying to ignore Howdy and the sense he seemed to be making. He was right. He needed to bring back the fear and what better way of doing it than taking revenge on the wankers that had done him over the night previous? He watched some kindly looking Irish gent shouting at two bawdy Aussies that they couldn't bring that many cigarettes and a koala into the country, while wondering if the border force TV shows were scripted. Surely they'd have been stopped at the other end?

He shook the koala from his thoughts and looked at Howdy. "So how then?"

Chapter 6

"What are we doing here?" Harold looked out the car window to the row of houses. They were small houses at the end of some street he didn't think he'd ever been up before. A little cul-de-sac. Quaint.

Howdy pointed to the house on the end of the row. They were all detached, but you could say that this one was the last before the houses started going back towards the main road. There was a pub on the corner, one that always looked a bit dirty. They weren't that far from Harold's house. Only a few streets down. Harold had always wanted to go in the pub, but had never plucked the courage to. Not on his own. Who went into pubs on their own? Alcoholics, that was who. And he certainly wasn't one of those.

"Pay attention," Howdy said, jabbing his finger at the house again. "That one."

"What one?"

"The one on the end. In the middle. Don't pretend you don't know what I mean."

Harold focussed back on the house. "Who lives there?"

"Man with a dog."

Harold turned his look from the house to Howdy. "Who?"

"Man with a dog. The one that disrespected you a hundred fucking times."

"So?"

"So? Revenge, my poor clown. Revenge."

Harold shook his head in disbelief. "What the fuck are you talking about?"

"You need practice, right?"

That was true. If Harold was going to take down the cunts that had cut him up, he was going to need at least a little practice.

"And this dude disrespected you, man. He dissed you."

That was also true. Harold had always wondered why he hadn't at least *pretended* to be scared. His dog had tried.

"No, man. Fuck the dog." Howdy laughed. "Well, you can if you want, but that wasn't what I meant. Christ, you've got a dirty mind, ain'cha?"

Harold was shaking his head. He didn't think he wanted to do that. No. Just a play on words. But that dog *had* pissed him off. He looked from Howdy to the house and then back again. "Fuck up that old man, you mean?"

"Yeah." Howdy's voice was low and quiet now. Sinister and daring. He had an edge there, one that said he wasn't fucking around at the same time as saying, *look, cunt, if you don't do it, I might*.

"I couldn't," Harold said.

Howdy looked him down. "Then why the fuck did you come out dressed like that?"

Harold looked down himself. He was in full clown get up. He looked in the mirror. Face painted. Howdy was right. Why the fuck had he come out dressed like that if he wasn't about to go on a revenge filled rampage?

Harold rushed around the path towards the driveway to the house. He hoped that Howdy was right. He'd hate to go through all this and find some little old lady lived there who had a heart attack finding a pissed off clown standing there at the door.

Maybe he shouldn't try the front door first?

He hurried from the street hoping no one had seen him. It was still very early to be out and about in this get up. Lunch time in fact. "Fuck a duck," he muttered to himself, his over sized feet slapping on the concrete as he half-ran as best he could in the costume. To the safety of the side of the house. No one could see him, there, nestled in the side-way betwixt the hedge and house. He stopped for breath.

Howdy was already at the end of the building, gesturing him forward to the rear of the house. Harold raised a hand to make him wait, while he got his breath back. When composed, he stood and slid carefully along the side of the building. Looking in the windows as he went. He could see that rat faced fucking dog. Fast asleep in a basket on the floor in the hallway. Fucking useless dog. He continued around. Couldn't see the old man anywhere. Hopefully he *was* there.

When he reached Howdy, he said, "He's upstairs." Then he nodded knowingly.

"Right," Harold said. He went to the back door and could see through the window that it led to the kitchen. He tried the handle. Motherfucker opened first time. No need to break windows or anything. Harold drew his fingers to a fist and bumped the air. Then saw the look of distain on Howdy's face, before he stopped and pushed the door open. The door from the kitchen to the hall was closed, and the dog had, so far, heard nothing. He slipped in. Looked back to Howdy who was standing on the edge of the grass, making shoo gestures, and not making any attempt whatsoever to join him.

Great. He closed the door, so the dog didn't get out. How was he going to do this? He stopped and focussed on himself for a moment, looking to find some centre. How? *How*? Why? Was he really going to do this? He'd broken into someone house. It was still breaking bad even if the fucking door *was* unlocked. But, he reminded himself, he had left the door unlocked, and this was the least he could do. He was, after all, just going to scare him, right? *Scare the shit out of him.* He glanced back at the door. It wasn't too late to bottle it.

"No," barked Howdy. "You cowardly little bastard." He turned his back and stared out the window into the garden.

Harold looked at the back of his head and then to the back door. Still closed. He wished he wouldn't do that.

"What?" Harold hissed.

"You have to make him sorry. Scare him. Scare the fucking balls out of him."

Harold nodded, "You're right, you're right," he placated. "I'm on it." He went to the door and slowly reached out to the handle. He just needed to get upstairs without waking the dog. His hand on the handle, he turned it. Just a fraction. The smallest amount of turning you could do without turning-turning the handle.

Then the barkening started.

Chapter 7

"Fuck." Harold pulled the door open and the dog stood its ground. It was at the bottom of the stairs, just outside its little bed. Barking for all its worth.

"Shut it up," Howdy snapped.

Harold didn't know what to do. Everything was going to go wrong if the dog didn't shut the fuck up. Old man what's-his-name was going to realise something was wrong and call the fucking police. So Harold did the only thing he could think of. It seemed natural in the situation, what with the size of the dog and whatnot. He took the two required steps forward, and with his over-sized clown shoes, punted the yappy little retard.

The dog yelped out something pathetic, and was launched—impressively, Harold would tell you—straight through the next door into the living room. It smacked against the wall. A sickly thud. And then slid, somewhat comically down the wallpaper. That wallpaper with the wood chips in it that only old people have. Coming to rest, serene and finally fucking peaceful on the carpet. Next to the old-person sideboard.

Howdy audibly chuckled. "Noice."

Harold shook his head. He could still hear the barking in there like it was a heart under the floorboards. "I didn't mean to do that."

"You *accidently* toe punted the dog to death. That's somehow more impressive." Howdy managed to sound enchanted, like Harold was something of a hero.

Harold shuddered it away. "Right. Scare the shit

out of the old man."

"Yesssss." Howdy did some sort of a jig, and made a bom-bom-bom, noise.

Harold shook his head and started up the stairs. For each step he could see the old man, lying on his bed, torn open, his guts slipping out to the floor, blood, hot and sticky, on the sheets, on the headboard. The man's eyes frozen in terror, held open in death. "Right," he muttered to himself ... "Right." He got to the top of the stairs and looked back for Howdy to be behind him, but he wasn't. He was at the bottom of the stairs looking happier than he even had, thumbs up, grinning. He was nodding Harold forward.

"Right," he muttered ... *again*.

He went to the first door on the landing, closed, and listened. Couldn't hear anything beyond, but if the old fucker was asleep, then he wouldn't, would he? He frowned. Snoring, maybe? He pushed the thought from his head and gripped the door handle, twisting it slowly and cracking the door. Beyond was a spare room. Done out to look like an office, computer sitting on the small desk that looked like it had come from a catalogue. The thing was on, left on. There was a picture of a naked chick on the screen. Harold could see it from the door. He sucked air in through his nose. He shouldn't. But he wanted to. Nay, perhaps, he couldn't help himself. He opened the door to the office and crept in, pushing it closed behind him, so he didn't disturb the old man, apparently sleeping in the opposite room. He went to the screen and peered at the nude figure. Asian. Young. Harold frowned. Right. *Okay*. He looked back at the door, thinking he'd heard something ... movement perhaps. Then he turned his attention back to the computer. Old Windows thing. Looked like it was at least two gen back. He crouched and looked at the face of the girl on the desktop. Puffing his cheeks out like a chipmunk, fucking girl looked *awfully* young. Probably because she was Asian, right? He bobbed his head from side to side. Could be because she was Asian. Some girls just have that look, don't they? Long into their twenties ... looking like a *kid*.

Harold's frown deepened. "Yeah," he said, quiet. He looked at the computer chair, a quick thought to sit in it, and then he discarded the thought as he became more disgusted at the thought of this old ... fucker. Harold was happy to call him a fucker for now. He touched the mouse, gently, and guided it to the Start button, opening the menu. He went to the Recently Used documents section, filled with pictures with names that didn't mean anything. He hovered the mouse over the top one. His finger shaking as he held it there, over the left hand mouse button, waiting. His tummy twirled a little. He wanted to know if this cunt was doing something he shouldn't have been. But also *he didn't*. Christ. What would he tell the police? Yeah, see, I was just in the neighbourhood when I accidently ended up in this geezers back bedroom, sitting on the computer, and I found a whole bunch of kiddie porn. Dressed as a clown. And, I toe punted his shit-dog, probably to death.

"Young 'un's, eh?"

Harold nearly shit when Howdy spoke. He turned and looked up at the clown. Stood over him. He was looking by the menu to the Asian girl on the desktop.

"Nice," he said.

"You're unbelievable."

"What?" Howdy sounded indignant. "She's probably of legal age." He looked over his shoulder. "What, you think that maybe ..." His eyes came back to Harold. "No. I mean, he seemed like such a nice old man."

Harold turned back to the screen. It was obvious, wasn't it? He was a fucking pedo. Out walking his pedo dog late in the evening, pretending to be a normy. He pushed himself back to stand and jumped again when he turned and found Howdy had already left the room. Harold went back to the old man's bedroom door. He suddenly wanted to know what his name was.

Taking the handle, he pushed the door open. There he was. On the bed. Splayed out a little. He was on top of the covers, the room was moist. Hot. Sticky. There was a smell in the air, one he couldn't quite put his finger on. He stepped in and looked at the man. His glasses were on the bedside table, head back, nose pointing to the ceiling with his mouth hanging half-open. He was wearing a vest and a pair of over-starched white boxers. The more Harold looked at him, the more he looked like a pervert. Harold glanced to the floor, his oversized shoes almost under the bed. Tissues littering the floor.

Oh, God. That was what the smell was.

Fuck.

He retched slightly, swallowing it back. Glanced back to Howdy sitting in the chair by the wardrobe. He was eating popcorn. "Scare him," he said.

Then the old man opened his eyes. "What the fuck?" he blurted, which was probably an understatement. I mean, what would you say if you woke up in the middle of a lovely nap to find a couple of clowns in your bedroom?

Harold blinked. Just once, the vision of the torn to pieces old man behind his eye lids, and then he saw red. Couldn't help it. It was inevitable. Once he'd seen the computer. Harold jumped on the bed, straddling the old man. He punched him in the face. Hard. He was still wearing his clown gloves, so he didn't think it would have hurt as much as he wanted it to, but he underestimated the fragility of *old man* consistency, smashing the fuckers face open like a ripe, bloody, tomato. His human gravy splattering out from the split across the bridge of his nose, running rampant, down into his mouth. It even cast an array of spots on Harold, himself. The old man's eyes, wide. Full of terror. He reached out, trying to claw at Harold, maybe, his fingers grasping at Harold's face, doing nothing, weak and pathetic. Harold hit him again, his blood smearing over Harold's gloves. He held him down and just stared at him for a moment. The thought of what he'd done ... just ...

He growled in anger.

Harold jumped from the bed and pulled the frail old man by his feet, dragging him from the mattress, his body hitting the floor, a hollow thump. Dragged him to the top of the stairs. Harold wrestled him to his feet, and looked into his eyes. "You make me sick," he muttered, pushing him onto the stairs, down.

The old man cried out as he left the floor, in mid-air for a moment. Flung. Fallen. Then that same hollow sound as he hit the carpet. Harold shouted, "*Fire in the hole*," and started down after the man, and he twisted and turned, crumpling into a sack of flesh and bones. He was crying when he hit the bottom. Harold wondered if he might kill him by doing that, but no. Which, as Harold felt the way Harold felt, was probably good. He was careful not to fall himself going down the stairs to the man. You know, with his oversized shoes. Damned tricky they are, going down the stairs.

He was weeping. Like a little school boy who'd had his favourite Transformer taken from him and thrown onto the roof of the toilet block. Harold winced at the memory. He stood on the man's arm, hanging useless to his side, and heard the bone breaking, splintering into two with his weight.

For a brief second the man's sobs got louder, and he seemed to tighten, pulling himself into a ball. But Harold was having none of it. "You motherfucking kiddie touching …" he paused, looking for the right word, "… cunt." *Yes*. That would do it. He hunched over his figure, and slapped him across the face like an Italian mobster in a b-movie. "Get up," he barked. "Get up and face me." He stood, himself, and paced for a moment, waiting for the old man to get from the floor. Which he didn't, enraging Harold even more.

"Go on," said Howdy, sitting at the top of the stairs. "Fuck him up."

Harold took him at his word, and strode back to the man, dragging him from his foetal position, out into the hallway, and starting to stomp on him. Big shoes. Big stomps. He started laughing, watching the old man squirm as footfall after footfall landed in random places on his anatomy. "Yes," he giggled, another foot landing upon his torso.

With each landing came a grunt, and the man twitched and curled. Muttering out words like *please*, and *no*.

Harold stomped on him a few more times, before grabbing him by the vest and dragging him clumsily from the hallway into the living room, dragging him across the carpet, leaving dark and rough burn marks. He dropped him in the middle of the rug in front of the open fire, dead and cold. Looked around for something to do.

The old man was heaving in sharp breaths, like he was struggling to breathe. Maybe a punctured lung or something.

Harold went to the far wall and picked up the dog. He took it to the old man and showed him. Through purple and red stained eyes, flesh billowing out, thick and painful, swollen, the old man looked at the dead dog and weeped out in horror.

"Tatters," the old man said. "Not Tatters."

"Stupid name for a dog," said Harold. He held the dog by its back legs like some dude-bro holding a fish for a photo, and then swung it, more akin to a pool ball in a sock, than a fish. He hit the old man with the dog-corpse, right across the head.

The old man screamed out, but weakly. "Help me," he screamed.

At least that was what Harold thought he screamed. Hard to tell really, as bone met bone, and the two ground together. The dog was the first thing to lose its head in all of this, though, as Harold swung it around, hitting the old man, over and over. Blood shedding across the room, liberal and wide. Some the old man's. Some the dogs, no doubt. The man's cries deadening as he too, deadened. The head came from the dog, as the bone broke and tore through the small dog flesh releasing its little tennis ball sized head to be free. Tossed to the spirit of itself to be caught on another plane of existence. More blood sloshing from it. Over the wallpaper (improving it, indeed) and the carpet and the old man, and Harold himself.

Until he stopped.

Stared down at the old man. His head caved in, bones sticking from his face. No more breath. A couple of death twitches, that was all.

Harold was breathing hard. He needed to improve

his circular vascular intensity, or whatever bullshit personal trainers spouted at you. He dropped the dog. Probably didn't have a set of weights that allowed for beating someone to death with a dog.

Howdy, sitting on the sofa, and remarkably free of blood, started to clap. "I thought," he said, "you were just going to *scare him*."

Harold looked at him. "He looked pretty scared to me."

Harold looked at the mail sitting on the side of the table by the front door as he left. It was all addressed to one *Mr. Rogers*. Very fitting, he was sure. He'd stop at a phone box on the way home and call the fuzz, anonymously, to tip off where the pedo corpse was. Then he looked down at himself. Plenty of the old pedo blood on him. Maybe he should go home and wash first.

He pulled the front door gently closed and hurried to the car, leaving huge footprints of blood on the tarmac behind him. Howdy was already sitting in the car. Waiting, as Harold got in.

He was grinning. "Nice job," he said.

Harold nodded, starting the engine as he looked around the cul-de-sac hoping no one was watching the deranged clown covered in blood coming from Mr. Rogers.

CHAPTER 8

"Tatters?" said Howdy.

"Tatters," confirmed Harold.

"You want to name yourself after a dog?"

"Indiana Jones did." He looked from himself in the mirror to Howdy, sitting on the side of the bath behind him. "Besides, it's a stupid name for a dog."

"It's a stupid name for a clown."

"It's time I had a name and it's going to be Tatters. Okay?"

Howdy shrugged, and turned his attention to the porn mag he was holding in his lap. "Nice tits," he said.

Harold wiped the last of Mr. Rogers blood from his face and rolled his head around inspecting his clown makeup again. Looked good. Tight. He crossed the bathroom and looked into the mag that Howdy was holding. "Where the fuck did you get that?" he asked. The woman in the centre of the magazine—the page Howdy was currently drooling over—had a woman called Hilda in the picture. The writing wasn't in English and she was doing something utterly despicable with what looked like a candelabra. Hard to tell, as Harold could only see some of it. "I didn't think you could have pictures like that in magazines," he said, absently wandering from the bathroom to the kitchen. He opened the cupboards and looked in. Wasn't hungry. He wanted a drink though. Something with a little bite.

"So what's next?" Howdy said, standing in the doorway.

"What? I suppose, well." Harold opened the

cabinet and stared at the cooking wine. All he had in, he thought. He looked at his hands. Ungloved they were as white as his face. Then his eyes dropped down himself. Naked apart from a pair of shorts. The washer going around in the corner. He picked up the bottle and a glass.

Howdy scowled, "Desperate much?"

Harold shook his head and went to the living room, slumping into the sofa and flicking the TV on. Babestation. Some grotesquely massive-titted woman writhing about on a Persian rug, trying not to show her snatch was tongue fucking a telephone.

"Yeah," said Howdy, as he followed from the kitchen. He planted himself on the chair and crossed his legs.

"Jesus," muttered Harold. "You pervert." He poured a glass of cooking wine and placed the open bottle on the coffee table without replacing the lid. Then changed the channel to something about pottery being made by amateurs. Took a swig of the wine. Not the best. No.

Howdy looked at him. "Wanker."

Harold snorted a laugh. "Yeah, *me*." Then he said, "Lol."

Howdy turned in the chair and uncrossed his legs. "So, anyway." He looked at the ceiling. "Who *is* next?"

Harold shrugged. He was more than a little confused by all of this, to be totally honest. He supposed he should go after the three bastards that had knifed him. Show them what for. After Mr. Rogers, he was feeling pretty good about taking them on, and they *had* started it, so it was totally justified.

"I still think you need more practise."

"Hm?" Harold looked over the rim of the glass to

Howdy. He was staring at the TV even though his body was facing Harold.

"I can't wank to this," Howdy said. "Go on, be a sport. Turn it back over."

Harold took another swig. "You can wank to this if you try hard enough." He grinned, his attention going back to the nice man on the TV.

Howdy dropped trou. "Okay then," he said.

CHAPTER 9

Harold looked out the window of the car at the house. "What the fuck are we doing here, then? These people have got nothing to do with anything." They were sitting in the car outside the Cundray's house.

"I want you to see something," Howdy said. He was staring out the window, the same as Harold. Looking at the house.

"What?"

"You'll see."

Harold went to open the car door. "But why am I dressed like this?" he asked. The door was near impossible to open with his massive clown gloves.

"Again," said Howdy, getting out the car. "You'll see."

Harold hurried over to the driveway, and in. It was eight in the morning. Still a little dark. Cold. The sun coming up over the house illuminating the grass. Needed work. Harold made a mental note that he'd need to contact them. Make another appointment to come and see them about that. He followed Howdy down the side of the property, and into the shadows. Stopping behind him, as he pulled a packet of cigarettes from somewhere and lighting one. He sucked hard on the cancer stick and blew the smoke out, in Harold's direction. "Those things'll kill you," Harold said.

Howdy gave him a look of disdain.

Then Harold said, "I ask again, what the fuck are we doing here?"

"Look," Howdy said, pointing through the window.

Harold sighed and trudged to the glass, staying to the side to ensure he wasn't seen. He pushed his nose up to it and peered through. He could see that little shit, Danny. He was standing at the doorway to a room, down the hallway. Harold's eyes darted about taking in the surroundings. It was fecking posh in there. He raised his eyebrows as Howdy said, "Focus, twat," and looked back at Danny.

"What am I looking at?" Harold whispered.

"Come on."

Harold looked from the window and to Howdy. He was plodding off towards the back of the house. He followed, tramping his way through the roses, back to the grass. Shit. He'll have to sort that out later. He hurried to catch up with Howdy. "That Danny's a right little fuckwad."

Howdy shot him a look and wiggled his finger at him, to join him at another window. Harold sighed. He tramped more of the flowers he had lovingly planted with his giant clown shoes and looked through the window.

It was the dining room. A large, heavy hardwood table. One of those old fashioned farmers side board things, with royal looking plates on stands facing outwards. You know the ones. The ones celebrating events that you weren't supposed to eat off. The ones old people bought when they came out and then wondered why they never gained in value. *Because they're tat, Barbara.* Like those coins that have a special event on, fifty pence coins that cost two pounds and postage—direct from the royal mint—that are, in fact never worth more than the fifty pence cover value.

Howdy hit him in the back of the head. A gent slap, like he was a broken record.

Howard continued to look around the room. There was a small digital radio in the corner. It was on, playing something that Harold couldn't hear. The door. Where little Danny (the cunt) stood, one of those hostess trolleys. And Mrs. Cundray. She was on the table, on her back. Naked from the waist down, her legs wrapped around a swarthy looking dude. He was topless. Rippling muscles. Firm body. Taut. You know the sort. His hair jet black and slicked back. He was wearing jeans, but, Harold assumed, with the fly open. Because he was definitely fucking Mrs. Cundray.

"The pool boy," Howdy said.

Harold frowned. First, he was torn by his own stupidity. All those times she'd asked him in. Probably wanted to fuck him silly. He looked at Danny. But Danny was watching, which was gross. And more than a little weird. He looked back at the two of them. The table was well made. It wasn't even rocking. There was a glass—a crystal tumbler—with brown liquid in it (brandy, of course) and it was barely moving.

Harold couldn't hear what was being said. Apparently they had very good double glazing. He looked around the edge of the window. Maybe even triple glazing. Howdy sighed, very audibly, and Harold returned his look to little Danny.

"Now you understand?"

Harold nodded, slowly. "Yeah," he whispered, watching Fabio the Poolboy as he put his hands behind his head and continued rhythm, his eyes closed. Mrs. Cundray clawing at his torso. "Danny is abused. He can't help the way he is. It's all ... it's all just a cry for help."

Howdy leant forward. "He's actually a bit of a

knob end, but this shit can't help, right? So you know what this means."

Mrs. Cundray seemed to be reaching some sort of crescendo at the end of her recital, and at that point, and only then could Harold hear her screams and wails of pleasure.

"I'll make her scream," Harold scowled.

He straightened from the window and stamped on some more flowers, before leaving the window and waiting, hidden from sight, at the side door to the house. The pool boy equipment was sitting there, around the pool, waiting for him to return.

It didn't take long. The door opened and Fabio came out. He pulled a packet of smokes from the back of his jeans and while he was lighting it, Harold slipped around behind him and into the house.

Closing the door silently behind him. He hurried around the kitchen and to the hallway. Suddenly face to face with little Danny. Well, face to crotch, because of the height difference, but that didn't really matter, now did it? Danny looked him in the eyes, his face was red and slippery wet from the tears. From being forced to watch his mum adulterate with a man that wasn't his father. Harold shook his head. The boy sniffed thick snot up into his nose, swallowing it back. "Who are you?" the kid whispered, not recognising Harold under the makeup.

"Name's Tatters, kiddo. Why don't you go and play in your room? Don't you come out now."

Danny nodded, scurrying away.

Knob end, Harold thought. He listened, waiting. Could hear some movement from the other room. He went to the door. There she was. Still on the dining table. Legs spread, facing the door. Facing Harold. She was hooked up on one elbow now, the glass of brandy in her hand. She glanced to the clown standing in the doorway. "I don't remember ordering you," she said, the words slurring from her mouth. She took another mouthful of brandy and swallowed it. Placed the glass down on the table next to her, and then lay back. She said, "Come on then, you can fuck me too."

Harold glanced down the hall to make sure Danny had disappeared, and then stepped into the room.

"Is it the boy's birthday or something?" she asked.

Harold frowned at her. Well, at her cunt anyway, as it was pretty much the only part of her he could see. Feet up on the table now.

"Maybe it's mine? Come on then." She giggled. "Fuck me."

Harold watched as some of the pool boy's goo slipped from her, down, onto the table below. What was it called? A custard pie, or something?

Well no *thank* you.

She lifted herself and looked at him, seemingly surprised that he wasn't already clown deep in her. "You want the boy here?" she asked. "That's okay. That's my jam too."

Harold drew breath in, and before she could scream for the child to come forth and observe the copulations, he thwhacked his hand over her mouth. She looked at him. The two of them, there, Harold between her legs, being careful not to get Fabio custard on his clown outfit, his hand over the woman's mouth. She was snorting air in through her nose. Harold realised she was touching herself, apparently leaning into the hand thing and thinking this was some sort of kink. Harold screwed his face up. He was so obnoxiously angry at that point he could have just screamed. He released her face, and she looked a little stumped for a second, before his hand darted up, to her hair, and grabbing a handful of it. Then he yanked. Hard. Spinning her in the liquid on the table. It wasn't just Fabio juice, you know. Some of it was hers, too. Then he dragged her, by the hair, from the table. Down to the floor.

She landed on her coccyx or something. Let out a scream, a wail, as she landed. Sounded no different to her screams of pleasure, so it shouldn't bring the boy, although, perhaps it might be an idea to let him watch this one. Cathartic. Harold dragged her to the hall, and across, into the kitchen. "Who are you?" she screamed between wails of pain and fear.

Harold let her go and turned, standing over her, upside down. "I'm Tatters the Clown, bitch," he said. It had sounded cooler in his head, but it was public now, so Tatters the Clown was the name he was sticking with.

"It a dog's name."

Harold glanced to Howdy, sitting on the kitchen counter. He had a chicken drumstick and was nibbling on it.

"Are you going to scare her, like you scared Mr. Rogers?"

"Yeah," Harold said. His eyes dropping down to Mrs. Cundray. She was looking at Howdy. Maybe.

Then her eyes returned to him. "You can fuck me," she said.

It threw Harold through a loop. Was this her bargaining for her life? You can fuck me? He could have done that already (gross) should he have wanted to. Did she think she was that? Like *all that*. That he could be bought of with custardy seconds from that ... that ... he looked out the window at Fabio. Standing at the poolside, rearranging himself in the front of his jeans.

Harold glanced to Howdy and reached over, swiping the chicken drumstick from him. He held it aloft (like a mighty sword) and plunged, while dropping to his knees. The fat end of the drumstick stabbed into the woman's whore-mouth and down, passing her non-existent gag-reflex, to her throat. Into her gullet. She muffled out a scream, clawing at Harold in a different way than she had Fabio. She choked and spluttered, spit coming out her nose. A hard cough and a little extra Fabio juice squirted to the kitchen floor. She was making this noise like an asthmatic sloth trying to hold onto a really tall tree, before Harold throat punched her.

Seemed fitting.

She stopped moving. He could see her neck flexing and stretching. Her hands still on his clown outfit. Her eyes slowly becoming more desperate. She couldn't breathe. At all. She was drowning in her throat, swelling around a chicken bone. Blocking her airways.

Harold said, "Ding dong," like Leslie Philips might, and then grabbed a knife from the counter. Stabbed it into her neck, not hard or deep. More of an experiment than anything else. He twisted it lightly and pulled it out. A small amount of blood squitted out, but the hole hissed, as she suddenly found air, him bypassing her mouth for her. Then she started to cough violently as she was filling with blood from the wound. Harold held her to the floor. He brought his knees up, over her shoulders and knelt on her. Holding her, pinned to the tiles. As she choked on her blood and squirmed and wriggled ... like a worm. Harold glanced around the counters, looking for something ... his eyes falling on the brandy bottle. He grinned, reaching out and managing to just touch it with his tippy fingers, slipping around the bottle slowly drawing it to him. He glanced to Howdy, watching from only feet away. "You could help," he whispered.

Howdy shrugged. "You're doing fine."

The bottle rolled around on its base a little and Harold finally managed to get his fingers on it, proper. He spun the cap off and turned it upside down. Quickly jamming the lip of the bottle into the neck hole of Mrs. Cundray. The liquid in the bottle sitting there for a moment, before the air in her lungs started to transpose with the sticky, burning liquid. The brandy flooding her airways as the only way she could breathe was beginning to drown her. She looked, wildly at Harold. He could see the fear.

He'd *brought the fear*.

He grinned at her and with his free hand, waved. Like a children's entertainer.

She began to convulse. There on the kitchen floor. Drowning in brandy.

This is really going to fox the police, Harold thought. He sniggered a little at first, and then begun to howl with laughter as the flailing of the drowning woman slowed to a stop. He was still laughing when she was laying there like a fish, pulled from the water, and gone.

"Nice," said Howdy.

Harold got from the floor and wandered the house for a few minutes, careful not to disturb the child. Danny. He looked at the ceiling, wondering if he should put him out of his misery. He was broken after all. His attitude … could it be fixed? Was he going to turn into a serial adulterer like his old mum? Harold shook his head. No way to know for now.

He stood, looking out the window. That Fabio motherfucker was still standing by the pool, smoking.

Harold shrugged it off. Well. That was another job done.

He went through the kitchen and opened the back door, stepping out. Fabio turned and looked at him. The two met eyes for a moment, and then Fabio, finishing his cigarette, flicked the butt away into the flowerbed.

Harold watched it land. He could feel this burning anger in him, rising up like lava. A rage, uncontrolled and without a leash. A hate that could never be bound. He looked from the butt to the bastard. "*You*," he scowled.

Fabio looked somewhere between concerned and confused, fronted with a clown, who was, for reasons unknown, extremely aggressive.

"*You*," he said again. Then he charged. A scowling screaming rising from him like a charging tiger. He threw himself at the pool boy and the two of them collided, Harold's shoulder hitting Fabio hard in the chest and the two of them careened backwards, stumbling, over the edge of the pool, into the water.

Harold lost all sense of sound, suddenly the world's noise damped by the water as he flailed to get upright. Fabio doing the same. Harold found the base of the pool with his feet and pushed himself up, breaching the water, and righting himself, just as the pool boy returned, also on the bottom, the two of them standing in the shallow end. Harold swung a fist out of anger, catching Fabio in the teeth. He stumbled, stunned, backwards, into the water, once again. Howard waded forward, grabbing him by the hair. At first glance this buffed out dude should have taken Harold in a blink of the eye, but Harold had surprised him in more ways than one and it certainly appeared that he was a lover, not a fighter. Harold walked him the two steps to the side of the pool and slammed his head forward, to the tiled pool's edge, bouncing his thick fucking cigarette smoking skull from it. There was a less than healthy, numbing, hollow crack and when he came back up, he stared into the middle distance like something really interesting was sitting there. A bit dull behind the eyes. There was a momentary pause, and then blood gushed from a split, previously unseen on his forehead. It spilled like tomato soup down his face and to his rippling torso below.

"My flower beds, you cunt," Harold shouted, dipping his head again with some effort into the side of the pool. His head split further open, revealing his super over sexed pea brain below. "Tell your friends Tatters sent you." Then Tatters slammed his head down the third time on the edge of the tiles. The ceramics digging into his soft smooshy brain, bits of it flinging out to the poolside, splopping into the water. Tatters let him go and he stood there for a second, dazed, blood and weird looking grey matter coming from the trench in his forehead, then he flopped into the water. Down. Then up. Bobbing. Tatters stood there. Staring at him as the water turned pink around him.

"So deffo going with Tatters?" Howdy said.

Tatters nodded. "Deffo," he echoed quietly. He climbed out of the pool and waited as his clown trousers emptied of water. "Now," he continued, "do you know where I can find those motherhumping bastards that jumped me in the park?" Tatters started back to the car.

Howdy followed. He raised a finger, "Well," he said. "Technically, you *were* going to jump them. I mean, I'm not one to say that you're in the wrong—"

Tatters turned and glowered at Howdy and he stopped talking. The two of them returning to the car in silence.

Chapter 10

"You're sure he lives here?" Tatters sat behind the wheel. The traffic had died down after eleven and now as they crossed the midnight hour, the streets were almost silent.

"Yeah," Howdy said, looking out the window to the Ferris wheel in the distance.

Tatters looked to the houses. Small terraced houses. He'd been in the type before. Two up, two down. Houses smaller than his basement flat. His eyes moved to the street. The road came out on the seafront, next to the arcades. And down that road, the run down amusement park. The great British seaside. Kids didn't want big wheels and spinning whirly things now. They wanted to go in the arcades for sure, but last time he'd seen, the arcade machines were like, two pounds a pop. Christ. You can buy games for less than that. He leant back in the seat and sighed. Or maybe he was just getting old. "So why don't we go and get him? Why the steak out?"

Howdy looked at him. "Stake."

"What?" Tatters grunted.

"It's stake out. Besides, we're not the police, you know."

Tatters shook his head. "Whatever. What would you call it then?"

Howdy ignored him. "I suppose you want me to go down to the seafront and get some donuts?"

"They're closed." Tatters tapped the clock on the dash. "After midnight." He looked back out the window. "Wanna kebab instead?"

"There." Howdy was pointing out the window.

Tatters squinted into the night. The streetlights in the area were shocking. It was a surprise that there weren't more accidents on the road. He might have been able to recognise him. Wasn't the leader, that was for sure. He glanced to Howdy. "You sure?"

Howdy was nodding, looking at Tatters now and not the creep. "Wanna get him now, or wait until he's inside. Then we can take our time?"

Tatters rubbed his chin. "Yeah. Maybe that one." The bastard was walking along with a weave in his gait. Been drinking. Or something else. He had a cut down denim over his leather jacket like it was the nineties, and his hair was a mess. He loped to the house and fumbled for an excruciating length of time with the key, before stumbling over the threshold and closing the front door behind him. "How are we getting in now?" Tatters asked.

"In through the back," Howdy replied. "Come on, Tats, let's get him." He was already opening the door and climbing out.

Tatters sighed. He really kinda wanted a kebab. Maybe later. He got out the car and followed Howdy across the road, wondering what it must be like seeing this escapade from a distance. This thug coming home in the middle of the night and as soon as the house door is closed a bunch of clowns pile out this car and go down the alleyway to the backs of the houses.

Lol.

Howdy disappeared into the shadows of the alleyway, and Tatters stopped at the mouth. It smelled like dog shit.

"It is dog shit," Howdy hissed from the shadows. "Come on, it won't kill you."

Tatters sighed and followed him in. He could *feel*

the shit as he stood in it. Dredging it along to the gate into the yard at the back of *Bastard*'s house.

"This one," Howdy said, his voice low and menacing. "Come on." He was already rattling the handle.

Tatters pushed him aside and opened the gate, slowly. Slipping his head through into the darkness beyond. There was a light on in the house, there facing them. The kitchen. He was there. Looked like he was staring straight at Tatter's head. The two stood for a moment, neither moving, until Bastard looked down and started doing something below the window.

"He can't see you out here," Howdy said, jabbing Tatters in the back with his finger.

He was right. He was probably looking at his own reflection in the glass.

"What's he doing?" Howdy asked from behind, gently pushing Tatters forward into the yard.

Tatters stepped in and waved at the man. Howdy was right. Couldn't see shit. That was why people needed curtains. You know, all those people in horror movies with their massive windows in the modern houses? Asking for it.

The two of them stood there, watching him roll a joint. Badly. He was super pissed.

"He's super pissed," Howdy said.

Tatters nodded along, wondering why Howdy kept pointing out the obvious. He watched. Waited. Eventually he finished, and turned out the kitchen, the light going off.

"That's it," Howdy blurted, lurching towards the back door and yanking Tatters by the arm.

Tatters followed along to the back door. "It's not like it's going to be open," he whispered.

"You heartily underestimate the stupidity of the

common criminal." Howdy pointed at the handle. "Go on. Try it."

Tatters reached forward, his eyes flicking from the handle to Howdy. He gripped the door handle and paused before turning it. Somehow, somewhere deep inside him, he knew that it was going to work. He smiled, as the door opened.

The smell of the house, beyond. "Jesus," Howdy said, pushing his hand over his mouth and nose.

Tatters agreed. It stank like old potatoes and cum. You know that smell. A teenager's bedroom. He stepped into the small hallway beyond. The door in front cracked open, light beyond. A small door to the right, probably a closet. He looked through the crack to the hall that led to the front of the house. The kitchen door to the left. There was a door to the left beyond the kitchen, light on, and a door to the right, light off. He looked around. Didn't fancy facing off against this guy, to be honest. He looked big. And he'd already bested him, even if it *was* with his mates. Tatters looked at Howdy, also peeping through the crack. And *he* was not much use. Tatters cracked the door open a little further. He could hear music coming from the door on the left. Good. He was smoking his joint and listening to some tunes. Perfect. Tatters pushed the door all the way open and entered the hall, creeping down to the door. He could hear the guy, in there, doing something.

Tatters looked around his feet. There was a baseball bat leaning against the wall. The weapon of choice for all thugs. So he grabbed it. Held it up. Howdy looked appreciative. Yes. This was the way to go. Tatters waited by the door, centring himself. Just getting himself in the right space before …

Tatters turned into the doorway.

The thug was standing in the middle of the room. He was facing the TV. Back to the door. There was an old fashioned stereo system—a stack system—in the corner blaring out some metal from the eighties, and he had the TV on, sound off. Joint gently smoking in his hand. There was some porn playing. He was naked.

His clothes discarded to the sofa.

His nude butt bouncing as he raised himself up and down on his toes in time with the on screen fucking.

Tatters frowned. He wasn't expecting … this.

Then the fucker must have heard—*sensed*—something, because he turned, facing Tatters, pointing with his *thing*. Erect and *ugh*. "Who the fuck?" he shouted.

It was only a small house. The neighbours probably heard that. So Tatters did what came to mind. The baseball bat, lifted from his shoulder, he brought it up, down, and then arced, a little like a golf club, teeing off the man's testicles.

The bat went up, straight between his legs and impacted hard on the sweet shop. The vibrations of the impact rising, up to Tatter's fingers, as he released the bat to the floor. The guy just standing there, staring. The music playing. The TV … fucking. Tatters reached down to his own junk and felt around looking for the bone he must have hit to cause that sort of vibe, and found one somewhere between his ballsack and his bum. Must have been that, that he'd hit. He sucked air in through his teeth, and grimaced at the guy, still standing. Mute.

His erection becoming flaccid, blood quickly starting to drool from the urethra. Like he was peeing blood. His left knee *went*, and he dropped to the side, collapsing without sound to the sofa. Eyes empty. Tatters wondered if he'd killed him. Seemed like an odd way to go. Then he started to shudder, to convulse, before wet and sticky bile plopped from his mouth, out to his chin, further, onto his chest, mixing in with the light ruff of hair he had there, bits of sweetcorn sticking in it. Gloopy and thick.

He then, finally, gurgled.

His eyes left the abyss and he looked at Tatters. Said, "I know you," weakly, before he started to move. Looked like he was going to try and get up to his feet. Tatters wasn't having any of that and stepped into a punt. Slamming his foot hard into the man's ribs, but rather than the pinking sound he expected to hear, that of the breaking of the bones, it was a smosh of cushiony softness.

He looked down at his clown shoes. *Stupid fucking clown shoes.* Then took a step back and leaned into a punch, his knuckles landing on the dickhead's chin. His head snapped back and he let out a grunt, but pain stroked up Tatters' arm from his fist. He waved his hand back and forth, massaging it with the other.

"What the fuck are you doing?" Howdy asked from the door, shaking his head.

"Oh, fuck off," Tatters hissed. He bent down and picked up the baseball bat, bringing it up and around like an axe this time, and bringing the smack down to his head, as he flailed about, trying to get up. The wooden bat cracked his skull clean open and his skin split. As Tatters raised the bat for a second go, Howdy rested his hand on his shoulder.

"Wait for it," he whispered.

Blood gushed down his face like he was the east face of Niagara Falls, into his eyes, his mouth, as he just sat there, staring. He suddenly said, "Cupcakes," and then his head lolled backwards to the sofa, the blood flushing down his bare torso and meeting his blood pee at the groin region.

Tatters glanced at Howdy. Howdy was invested in the TV. His head bobbing up and down at the sight of this dudes arse as he was going to town on ... well, it was hard to tell if it was another dude, a girl, or otherwise. Anal, though. Deffo anal. Tatters slapped him with the back of his open hand. "I want the next one," he said quietly.

Howdy looked from the porn to his face. He smiled slowly. "You're enjoying this aren't you?"

Tatters looked at the ballsack of the dude on TV and then the corpse of the guy on the floor. He bobbed his head from side to side. Yeah, kinda. He smiled to himself. Good to let out some stress.

He gave the guy a quick kick, just to be sure, and then stooped down and retrieved his joint from the floor. Took a quick toke, before dropping it back from whence it came. Be a shame if it were to burn the house down.

The two of them hurried back through the house to the yard, and out, to the car. Sitting there, outside the house, Tatters asked again, "Where to now?" He stared out the front window at the night, not looking to Howdy for the answer. Then he added, "I can smell dog shit."

He could. It was on his feet.

Chapter 11

"He lives here?" The house was huge. The second of the bastards lived here, on the posh estate on the outskirts of town. He was a rich kid. *Dick*.

Howdy was nodding. "Yeah. One of those *parents gives him everything and he does what he wants* sort." He looked down the road. "Fuck me," he said. "There he is."

Tatters followed his look, down the street. There he was indeed. Must be coming home from the same place as the last one. Yes. He was one of the two in the back. Same as the last one. Do for this one, and then get the leader. Tatters turned the key and started the engine. He put the car into gear, watching this wanker weave down the road.

He raised the clutch and started to move the car, slowly forward, front on to him. Lights off. Like fucking Knightrider or something. Then he had the music to Knightrider playing in his head.

The Hoff.

Cool.

He raised the clutch and dropped the accelerator hard, the wheels at the back spinning out and the car lurching forward wildly.

"Jesus fucking Christ," shouted Howdy as the two of them careened forward.

The car mounted the path, Tatters barely in control, the world suddenly turning in slow motion. Tatters could, in the blink of an eye, imagine what this cunt could see—this shitty old motor, suddenly bouncing up the kerb, two terrified looking clowns with their faces smooshed up the windscreen, screaming in fear.

Then his blink finished, time returned to normal, and the bastard slapped down on the bonnet, his legs dangling uselessly from the front of the car, his torso held via g-force to the bonnet, him and Tatters looking into each other's eyes like star-cross lovers (if one of them was a clown intent on *murder*).

Paying little attention to where the car was speeding, it was little wonder that it came to an abrupt halt when it hit a brick wall.

A blackness overtook Tatters, his head resting on the steering wheel. He opened his eyes and stared through the wheel at the console. All the lights were on. Like the oil light and the check engine light.

He raised his head, pain thumping behind his eyes. He looked in the passenger seat. Empty. Fuck. What the fuck had happened? The windscreen was smashed, cracks and shit where the safety glass had stopped it from shattering, but he could see the wanker on the bonnet.

Oh yes.

"Got him," Howdy said.

Tatters glanced to him. He was bleeding from a cut on the forehead. Wasn't wearing a seat belt, of course. Fucking clown. He jabbed his finger at the guy on the bonnet. The car holding him there, his legs shattered betwixt car and wall.

"Bleeding out," he said. "Look."

Tatters squinted, but couldn't see. He wound the window down and stuck his head out. Howdy was right. Everything below the hips was a ground up mess of blood and flesh and meat and bone. All pasted together like chicken liver pate. The guy was just laying there on the bonnet. We'll say *sleeping*.

The sound of another car got Tatters attention and

he looked down the street. Shit. There was someone coming. He pulled his head back in and tried to start the engine. It just weakly and sickly rolled over.

"Fuck that," said Howdy trying to open his door. "*Scarper.*"

The two clowns forced their way from the car and started to run down the street, away from the body and the car and the fucked wall.

Like an out of shape and somewhat delusional Batman and Robin.

CHAPTER 12

"Now what?" wheezed Tatters, hands on his knees, as he stared down into the pool of his own vomit. The price he paid for *running*. He sucked much needed air back into his lungs and looked at Howdy who seemed less worse for wear than he. "You could at least pretend to be suffering the consequences of a light jog."

Howdy glanced at him. "Oh, sorry." He held his chest. "*Oh,* that was *such* hard work," he said. He pushed his hand into his clown trousers and pulled a pack of smokes. Lit one. Immediately forgetting he was exhausted and returning his look to a displeased Tatters. "Only one of those fuckers left," he said.

"Where?" Tatters pulled himself to stand. "How are we going to get there without a car?"

"Come on." Howdy waved him forward and the two of them started walking.

They weren't that far from Tatters' tunnel. The scare tunnel. Call it what you will. "You telling me that this fuck head only lives around the corner from me?"

Howdy shrugged. "I guess."

The two of them by-passed the tunnel on the side of Harold's flat, and took a right at the junction, through a set of traffic lights and across the front of the cemetery. "Is it much further?" Tatters asked.

"Stop whining," barked Howdy. "You're the one who crashed the car."

Tatters didn't think he was whining, to be honest. And that wasn't very nice of Howdy to say, was it? He looked at the back of the clowns head as he walked a few feet in front like a teenager, embarrassed to be seen walking with his kid brother. They were on the narrow path going out to the farms.

Then Howdy stopped. At the opening to farmland. "Here," he said.

Tatters pulled up next to him. He looked through the gate. "I don't get it," he said. "There's no house here."

"Nope."

"I thought we were going to where the last one lived."

Howdy sighed, letting the air vibrate his lips at the air rushed through. "Yep," he said.

Tatters could hear the frustration.

Howdy climbed the gate, dropping down into the mud beyond.

Tatters followed.

Chapter 13

Howdy pointed. In the far corner of the field. A small caravan. It was blocked up on bricks and had graffiti on the outside. Picture of a willy. That sort of thing.

Tatters stopped walking and looked at the building. More of an outbuilding, to be honest. It looked like a fucking toilet. "He lives here?" he half whispered.

Howdy looked at him with a sadness in his eyes. A clown, crying.

Tatters nodded. "Well," he said. "Sucks to be him."

Howdy snorted out a laugh and then stopped himself. "So we're at that level," he said. Hushed. The two of them silent as the night that surrounded them as they walked over to the building.

As they got closer, Tatters could smell it. Smelled like a urinal cake. Very pleasant. "It's no excuse is it?" he muttered to himself. He wasn't sure if he was trying to persuade himself or not. He was sure, that living like this was no excuse to be a cunt, but that was how this had played out played out, hadn't it? This dude was a complete wanker and he was going to pay for it. Just like the rest of them.

Their mighty leader.

He smirked to himself, gave a quick glance to Howdy who was stood there, in the mud, watching him.

"Enjoying yourself?" he asked.

Tatters sort of rocked his head non-committedly from side to side.

"Good," hissed Howdy. "It's about time." He

smiled. "What's the plan?"

Tatters didn't know. He was just looking at the caravan. There was a small light, in the crack of one of the windows. Behind the curtains. He was in there. Probably doing drugs or some shit. Maybe he had company. Tatters' smile dropped. Shit. That was a good point. What if there was someone else in there? He didn't want to fuck up some innocent poor girl. Or boy. Sheep? Could be anything. He walked to the side, peering through the darkness to the other side of the caravan. Then he approached. Crept up on the crack in the curtains. He pushed his clown face against it. The crack wasn't large enough for him to be seen from the other side, he was sure.

He could see the bed. There were tea-lights resting on available ledges. That was where the light was coming from. He strained his head around trying to see more. Then something blocked his view. Someone had moved in front of the window. Balls. He pulled back a little to see more, and realised he was staring straight into the wrong end of a butthole.

Oh God. That cunt's arse.

Then it moved (thank fuck) and he pushed up close again. No. It wasn't the cunt's arsehole, but rather his guest's. The butthole in question was that of a young lady. Howdy pushed from behind. "Let me see," he hissed as Tatters pushed his eye closer to the gap, the young woman spreading herself over the bed. She was thin. Gauntly so. It was probably not the right conclusion to jump to, but Tatters assumed *meth*. That was good for weight-loss … wasn't it? Either way, she wasn't wearing a lot. A sheer shirt thing. Nothing else. He could see everything. Even through the sheer shirt, although that was probably the point.

"Let. Me. See." Howdy shoved Tatters out the way, and not wanting to alert the girl, he moved to the side, and huffed. Fucker.

"Yes," Howdy whispered. "I bet she's a goer."

"Goer?" Tatters tried giving Howdy a small push to see if he was going to move out the way, which he wasn't.

"Yeah. I think she's alone, too."

Tatters turned back into the field, squinting into the near perfect dark. "You mean he's out here?" He wasn't talking to Howdy, more to himself.

"We need to get rid of the girl," he said. "Jump him when he comes home."

That was a pretty solid idea, actually. "Yes," said Tatters.

"Can we fuck her?" Howdy asked, finally turning from the window.

Tatters frowned at him. "No." He nodded towards the door. "Come on. It's probably open." He hotfooted it to the door and took the handle, turning it and pulling it open. Pushing his way clumsily into the caravan.

The meth addict naked chick curled her face up like a scream queen and squealed, causing Howdy to push by and run at her. He brought his hand up like he was going to start fucking her up, when there was a crash from behind Tatters. He turned, finding the leader of the pack behind him. "Fuck," he blurted, just in time to see a fist hammer into his face. His nose honking, as the knuckles contacted his nose bone beneath and Tatters stumbled backwards, falling over the edge of the bed and landing in between the girls open legs. He was facing the leader. Standing there, waving his hand back and forth like it hurt. Well, Tatters thought, *he hoped it did*. He looked to

Howdy, now standing beside the bed, watching. "Well?" he asked. "Get him then."

He'd come from the toilet behind the front door. That was why they couldn't see him. Probably should have thought of that before barging in, but it was too late for hindsight. Tatters pushed himself from the bed as the meth addict had managed to get herself enough together to ask why there was a clown in the caravan, and he charged across the narrow space, hurling himself onto the wiry frame of the man. The two of them crashed into the kitchenette, spilling a pot of hot water to the side, down to the floor, the pot hitting the floor. Scolding water covering the two of them.

He barked, "*You*," at Tatters.

Tatters wondered in that split second who he thought it might be? Does this sort of thing happen often, clowns busting in in the middle of the night to start a barney?

Then he spat in Tatters' face. A full gob load of sputum. Some even went in his mouth. Tatters' stomach rolled as he tasted the spit of the man, his hands squirming as his blood filled his clown nose and pooled out, over the top, mixing with bastard spit and stringing down to his face, the two of them sharing fluids. Tatters pulled himself up to sit and pimp slapped him. His head snapping to the side— possibly out of surprise. "Beep-beep," Tatters shouted. Then he lunged forward in one glorious headbutt, slamming his head down into his nose. The man's grape nose split open and blood gushed out to his face, momentarily blinded, as Tatters reached around the counter top, looking for something, some weapon. He grabbed the first knife he came to and drew it up, over his head and plunged it down into his shoulder. The blade going straight through, into the floor of the caravan beneath, impaling him to it.

He screamed out in pain. Legs kicking out as he squirmed, one hand reaching out to Tatters, the other held limp, the muscles and tendons of the shoulder torn through and sliced up.

Tatters pulled himself back from the man, scrabbling to his knees, and turning. Checking to make sure that the meth addict hadn't gotten from the bed, and was coming at him. She wasn't, and Howdy was just leaning his arse against a cupboard trying to work out how the crack pipe he'd gotten a hold of worked.

The girl was still sprawled liberally over the bed. Legs spread. Fanny on show. *Nice jubblies*, Tatters thought, glancing over her body. He sniffed blood back into his nose and squeezed his clown nose, the honk dull and wet, and blood ejecting from it, over his face, to his lips, chin. "You should go," he said to her.

She looked … surprised … but not overly turned off. Eyebrows up. "My clothes," she said, like a wally.

Tatters shook his head. "Well, collect them up and get."

She nodded, pushing herself from the bed. She stooped down picking up what looked like random articles of clothing, before hurrying to the door (stepping over Bastard's legs as they flailed about). She stopped and looked at him, her clothes bundled into her arms, covering her breasts—although she didn't seem overly bothered by her beef counter being on display. "Call me, Bobby," she said, before turning out the door and off, into the darkness.

Tatters glanced down at, apparently, Bobby, and

then to Howdy. "Are you going to do anything to help me?"

Howdy looked from the pipe to Tatters and then shrugged, fishing in his pocket. He was either looking for a lighter, or he was playing trouser billiards. Knowing Howdy, it could have been either. Tatters fished in his own pocket and pulled his lighter. He handed it forward, and Howdy took it, nodding his thanks. Then Tatters turned back to Bobby. "So," he said. "What to do with you."

Bobby made this scream of anger and anguish before centring himself (as much as he could being somewhat nailed to the floor) and saying, "What the fuck do you want? Money?" His sniffed his blood into his nose, trying to look hard, but the illusion was shattered when it caused him to sneeze.

Tatters shook his head. Tutted. Made sure he looked properly authoritarian, as his eyes wandered the caravan looking for something suitable to do with … Bobby.

"My boys are coming over soon," Bobby expunged. He sneered like he still had the upper hand, when in fact he had no hand at all. "They're gonna *kill* you."

Tatters crouched. "No they're not," he said. "I've got one of them with their brain …" he laughed, "…what I could find of it, leaked all over the floor, and the other is pinned to a tree just outside his house. Very, very dead." He stood back up and stepped around Bobby, sticking his head in the toilet cubicle. He picked up the bottle of bleach and took it with him back to the main room. Howdy was smoking crack now, so he was busy. Tatters put the bleach down on the counter.

"What are you going to do?" Bobby's eyes darted

between Tatters and the bleach.

Tatters waved it away. "Oh don't worry about that. That's far too good for you." He pulled his clown costume up and showed Bobby his knife wounds. "You stabbed me," he said.

Bobby nodded. He was beginning to look terrified, to be honest. "I did," he said quietly. "So many times."

Tatters stepped from the caravan and looked out into the field, jumping himself down into the mud, and making sure the girl was gone. Then he rounded the caravan to the front. Where the tow bar had rotted off. He looked at the canisters. One of natural gas. That was no good. That might blow up. He scratched his head and rearranged his clown nose, his real nose beneath, aching. It made a clicking sound like this bastard had fucked it up good. That bird in the café was never going to look at him twice now, was she? He sighed, picking up the container of paraffin and lugged it back into the caravan. Must have been several gallons of the stuff. He looked at Bobby. "And why the hell you got this?" he said.

Bobby made some weird grunting noise. "What the fuck are you gonna do?" He screamed. "*What the fuck are you gonna do?*"

He sounded just like Brad Pitt in Seven. *What's in the box? Wah. Wah.* He looked at Howdy who was chuckling at the thought. Then he started sloshing the paraffin in the can listening to it. Good amount in there, there was. He twisted the cap off, and smelled it. A slight, subtle nothingness. "Right-o," he said. Then he started to splash the shit over Bobby, flailing on the floor, pulling with some more urgency now.

His feet kicking, hollow sounding, on the floor of the caravan. "Fucking no, man," he pled. "Jesus fucking you can't do this, man." The fear in his words becoming stronger. Taken, by some terror. "I didn't mean to man."

Tatters tossed the empty container to the hard wooden based sofa. You know the one all caravans had. It had the storage underneath.

Howdy stepped up next to him. His eyes, pupils, ballooned out, messed up. *Still* holding the crack pipe. "You gonna burn him?"

Tatters didn't take his eyes from the scumbag, writhing on the floor. Trying to get free, his blood pooling in the paraffin on the carpet beneath him. Shit caravan carpet. Trying to pull the knife from his shoulder. The blade, slipped in nice between the bones. Just by the clavicle.

Like his life depended on it.

Tatters took his lighter back from Howdy. "Yeah I'm gonna burn him." He rolled the thumb wheel of the thing, it making that crackling sound of the metal on flint. The spark as it thought about lighting, but didn't quite. The smell of the gas from the container below joining the light smell of the paraffin and the stench of pennies from the blood.

Bobby screamed. Again. *Louder.* Piss pooled on the front of his jeans.

Tatters rolled the lighter again and this time the flame bloomed. Hard, bright in the half-light of the caravan, burning with intensity greater than any of the fucking tea-lights surrounding them. He looked past the yellow flicker to Bobby. He had his fingers wrapped around the hilt of the blade and looked like he might have just realised that it was now or never.

Never, thought Tatters.

He dropped the lighter and suddenly the whole world was ablaze.

CHAPTER 14

The hollow *whump* of the paraffin taking was deafening, and the flames tore across nearly fucking everything. Tatters, thrown back, landed hard on the floor at the base of the bed where the whore was. A burning pain wrenched up his back and into his shoulders, a dullness in his head, where thoughts used to be.

Howdy was laughing, standing close to the flames. The small space filling with smoke.

Tatters pushed himself to his elbows, from the floor, sticky with ... um ... something. He looked at the fire. Bobby, still thrashing, flames licking him from head to toe as he burned. The wall of flames covering the floor, the walls, the door, gone.

He may have misjudged the need for so much paraffin.

Rolling to his knees, he pushed himself to his feet, watching the flailing burning man kicking and screaming, the acrid smoke burning his own throat. He looked around. No exit. Howdy was laughing so hard at the sight of Bobby, he was hunched over forward, his hands resting on his knees.

Tatters looked at the window. It was the only option. He'd seen the State do this in loads of stuff. He took a breath in, stupidly, in some preparation, hacking his guts up immediately after, the smoke stabbing at him. Then he charged. To the window. He knew what to do. Curl into a ball. Like a stunt man in a western. Thrown through the window of the local tavern or whatever.

He launched himself—not realising what a big

ask that sort of manoeuvre was—and crashed through, out to the field.

His expected landing and roll became more of a crumple, and he stopped dead in the mud. The flames licking the outside of the caravan, the air filled with the screams of Bobby. Christ he was making a meal of it, wasn't he?

The world darkening around the edges as he fought to stay conscious.

Howdy grabbed his hand and lifted it from the mud, pulling him from the side of the caravan out into the darkness. "Come on, Harold," he said quietly. "One more."

"What time is it?" Tatters asked. He was shivering. Dark. The two of them standing in the entrance to the industrial estate. The one down the road from the flat. Around the corner from the park. The one opposite the café.

"Five in the morning."

The road was still. The town not awake yet. "Why are we here?" Tatters looked around. The short row of closed shops. The café in darkness. The industrial estate empty. Devoid of life.

All except the faintest of clicks. Clacks. In the distance. Tatters squinted through the darkness, the streetlamps lighting virtually nothing. A woman, walking the streets, at that time. Alone. Tatters recognised her. The woman from the café. The Family Five. The girl. Whatever. "What?" he whispered. "What are we doing here?"

"Her," he said. Pointing.

"Her what?"

"Fuck her, or eat her guts or something."

Tatters looked at Howdy. "You've got to be

kidding me." He shook his head. Glanced back to her. She was opening up the café. Going in. The lights inside flickered on with a shudder, and he could see her once again. "No."

Howdy grabbed the back of his neck and started to push him forward, from the safety of the industrial estate, across the road, like a parent leading their unruly child to the headmaster. He frog marched him to the kerb, up to the wide paned window of the joint and pushed his nose up against the glass. "Her," he scowled.

She was looking at him. Nose against the glass. Staring through into the café at her. She looked scared, and Tatters could see her eyes darting back and forth from the door to him. Like she hadn't locked it.

"Right," Howdy pulled Tatters from the window and shoved him to the door. "Come on, Harold."

He pushed him against the door. It opened, he stumbled against the first table, looking at the girl. Eyes full of apologies. "Sorry about this," he mumbled.

Howdy was blocking the door. "Do it."

Harold looked from Howdy to the girl. She looked like she might shit, to be fair. Maybe already had. "No," he replied. "I won't."

"You have to," he barked.

Harold panicked. No. He didn't want to. This bird didn't deserve this. She didn't. Not just because she thought he was weird or something. Christ, she probably didn't even know who he was dressed like this. He turned on Howdy. "No," he barked back this time. He charged Howdy, colliding with him, clowns falling asunder from the doorway of the café.

As the two of them crashed to the damp early

morning path, he heard the girl slam the door of the café. Hopefully locking it. Good. She was safe.

Harold rolled to the side, taking Howdy with him, the two of them tumbling over each other, heads bouncing from the concrete.

"You can't turn on me," Howdy hissed, throwing a punch into Harold's mouth, suddenly raised up on his knees. "I *am* you."

"No," Harold blurted, pushing his way out from under Howdy. He slipped from the kerb, into the gutter. "You're not."

"I am an extension of your very being." Howdy was up. On his feet. Coming over to Harold. He lay a clown foot into his guts.

Harold howled in pain as his felt his insides shift about. His ribs cracking.

"You're a victim of being small …" he continued. Another kick, this time to the face. "… nothing without me." He kicked him again. *And again.*

Darkness shadowed over Harold's vision as he tried to roll into a ball. To protect himself from Howdy's persistent onslaught. Kick after kick.

He felt the old stab wounds start to re-open. Blood slicking out onto his clown costume. His this time. Weaker. Darker. Harold fought to stay awake. "Why?" he muttered. "You can't hurt me," he cried.

"Yeah we can." The three of them laughed.

"I'm *you*."

"Fuck you."

Then it stopped. All of it. And Harold lay there. Bleeding. He slept, he thought, for a few moments, perhaps. Lights firing behind his eyelids. A dullness in his thoughts.

Cold overcame him.

The cold hard path beneath him. Damp. At time went slowly forth. He opened his eyes a little. The tunnel. He could see the tunnel. His balloon, caught on a branch. The laughing of the three of them as they walked away from him. Leaving him there in the park. Harold spit up some blood.

Howdy the Magnificent was gone.

> Nothing more than an extension of me.

About the Author

Ash is a British horror author. He resides in the south, in the Garden of England. He writes horror that is sometimes fantastical, sometimes grounded, but always deeply graphic, and black with humour.

www.ashericmore.com

Printed in Great Britain
by Amazon